DATE DUE		
3-12-91	3-26	
5-7		
5-15		
9-15		

For Alistair and Danny
A.M.

For Alexander
P.L.

13541

First published 1987 by Walker Books Ltd

Text copyright © 1987 by Adrian Mitchell
Illustrations copyright © 1987 by Priscilla Lamont

Requests for permission to make copies of any part of the work
should be mailed to:
Permissions, Harcourt Brace Jovanovich, Publishers,
Orlando, Florida 32887.

Library of Congress Cataloging-in-Publication Data
Mitchell, Adrian, 1932-
Our mammoth.
Summary: The Gumble twins discover a mammoth frozen inside an
iceberg at the beach and take it home for a pet.
[1. Mammoth–Fiction. 2. Twins–Fiction
I. Lamont, Priscilla, ill. II. title.]
PZ7.M6850u 1987 [E] 86-26939
IBSN 0-15-258838-8

Printed in Italy
First U.S. edition 1987   A B C D E

Our Mammoth

Written by
Adrian Mitchell

Illustrated by
Priscilla Lamont

HARCOURT BRACE JOVANOVICH, PUBLISHERS

SAN DIEGO NEW YORK LONDON

We are the Gumble Twins,
Bing and Saturday Gumble.
Bing is a gloomy boy.
Saturday is a cheerful girl.
We get along fine.

One day we took a bus to the beach.
There was nobody else on the sand.
"The wind's too wild," said Bing.
"The water looks warm," said Saturday.
So in we went.
The sea was green and cool.
The waves were tall and bumpy.

Suddenly a mountain stood up in the sea -
   a blue and silver mountain.
A floating mountain of ice.
"It's an iceberg!" we shouted together.
It was our first iceberg.

The waves bumped the iceberg
        onto the beach.
"It's too slippery to climb," said Bing,
    "we'll break our backbones."
"I'll race you to the top," said Saturday.
So we climbed to the top of the
        slippy drippy iceberg and we
        looked down into the ice.

At first we wished we hadn't looked:
    we were as scared as skittles.
Deep down in the ice we saw two eyes.
Two big eyes, all brown and golden.
Two eyes, gazing up at us.
Our legs wanted to run away
    but our heads wanted to stay.
So we stayed and we stared.

The iceberg was melting
    faster and faster.
Out of one end
    came two curving tusks.
Then Saturday said, "Look -
    an elephant's trunk."
"Can't be," said Bing.
    "It's too big and too hairy."
We were too excited to
    be scared any more.
We blew on the iceberg to make
    the ice melt faster.

Soon all the ice had dripped
    into the sand.
There stood something,
    big as a bus.

"It looks like a hill," said Bing.
"A hill with hair instead of grass,"
    said Saturday.
"A hairy hill," we said together, and
    we knew it was really a mammoth,
    our first mammoth.

Our mammoth shivered and shook
    itself like a dog after a swim.
We jumped and squeaked.
Our mammoth stopped shaking.
It looked up at the sun.
It raised its trunk,
    then it trumpeted happily.

Our mammoth's hair was reddish-brown.
Our mammoth's hair was strong like string.
"Hello, Mammoth," we said.
It sniffed us with its trunk.

"It seems to like us," said Saturday.
"You never know," said Bing.
We climbed up the side of our mammoth.
We sat in the long, soft hair on its back.
We were high up in the air.

Our mammoth made
   a deep purring sound.
Then it started to walk
   over the sand.
We steered our mammoth
   by its ears to the field where
   we live in a trailer.
We were so happy
   we sang all the way -
"Here we come on our mammoth."
When cars hooted at us
   our mammoth hooted back.

When the mammoth saw our mom,
Sally Gumble, it raised its trunk and
gave a joyful honk.
The honk made our mom jump.
"Bing and Saturday, what on earth is that?"
"It's our mammoth," we said.
"We found it in an iceberg on the beach."

"Your mammoth is not an *it*," said Mom,
      "your mammoth is a she.
She was frozen into that
      iceberg many years ago.
She must be hungry.
What do mammoths eat?"
We didn't know
      but our mammoth knew.

The field was full of buttercups.
Our mammoth gave a snorty noise.
She picked two hundred buttercups
   with her trunk.
She popped them in her mouth.
She munched them up and
   gulped them down.

"Can we keep her?" we asked.
"Of course we can," said Mom, "she's beautiful.
What shall we call her?"
Bing said, "Sandie, because we found her
    on the beach."
Saturday said, "Hilda, because she looks
    like a hill."
But in the end we named her Buttercup.

Mom found a very old book in a shop.
It was called

How to Look After Your Mammoth.

It told us how to make Buttercup Pie.
The three of us ate a little of the pie
    but Buttercup ate a lot.